To: ....

From: ....

GROSSET & DUNLAP
An Imprint of Penguin Random House LLC, New York

Published in the United States of America in 2021 by
Grosset & Dunlap, an imprint of Penguin Random House LLC, New York.
GROSSET & DUNLAP is a registered trademark of Penguin Random House LLC.
Manufactured in China.

Visit us online at www.penguinrandomhouse.com.

www.mrmen.com

The publisher does not have any control over and does not assume any
responsibility for author or third-party websites or their content.

ISBN 9780593224144   10 9 8 7 6 5 4 3 2 1

MY TEACHER
and me

by Roger Hargreaves

Grosset & Dunlap

My teacher is
no ordinary
teacher.

They have a magical way of making learning fun.

My teacher is as wise as an owl.

And as clever as Mr. Clever.

I don't think there is a book my teacher hasn't read.

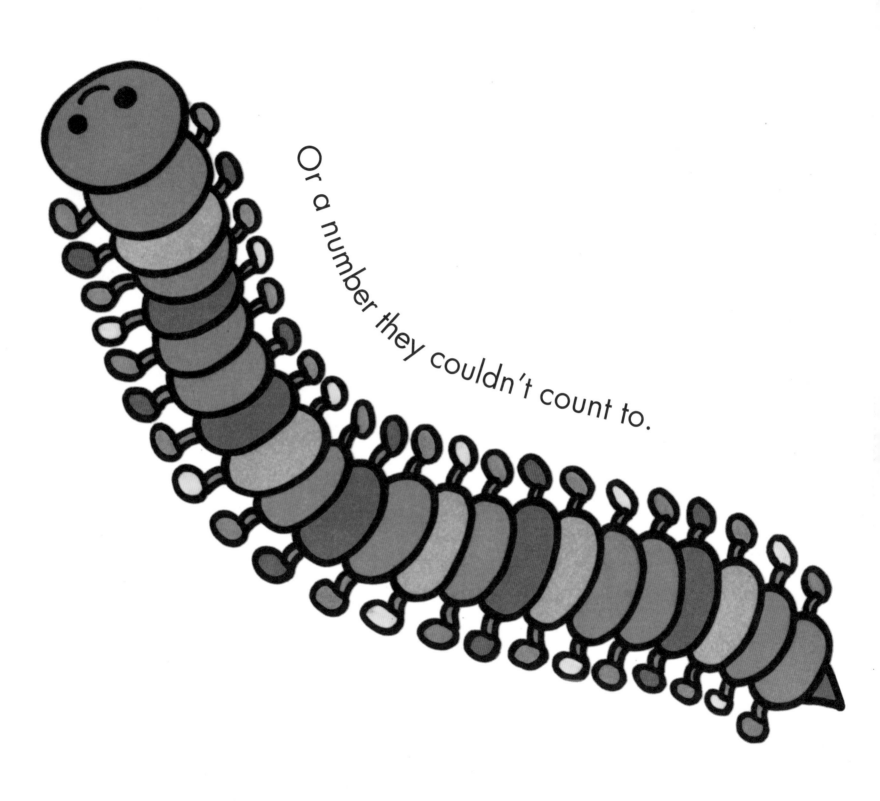

Or a number they couldn't count to.

My teacher is so much fun and knows
how to make me smile.

There are no bored faces in our class!

My teacher's stories take my class to other worlds.

And they encourage
us to see things in a
different way.

Sometimes I've felt a little shy.

But my teacher has given me confidence and helped me to shine.

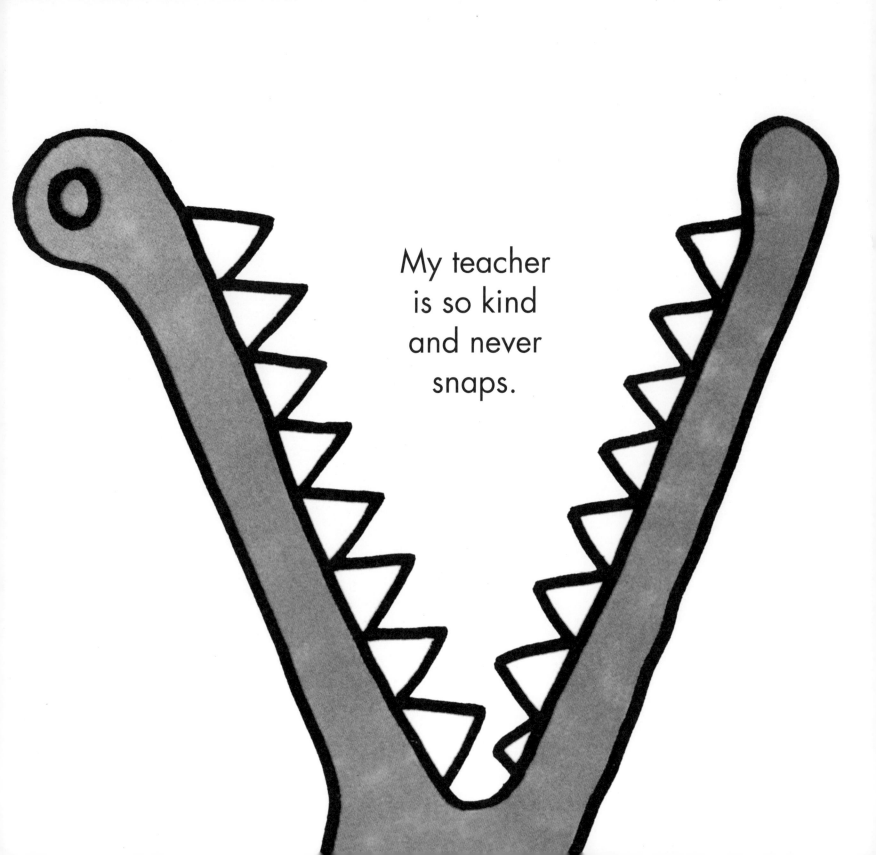

My teacher
is so kind
and never
snaps.

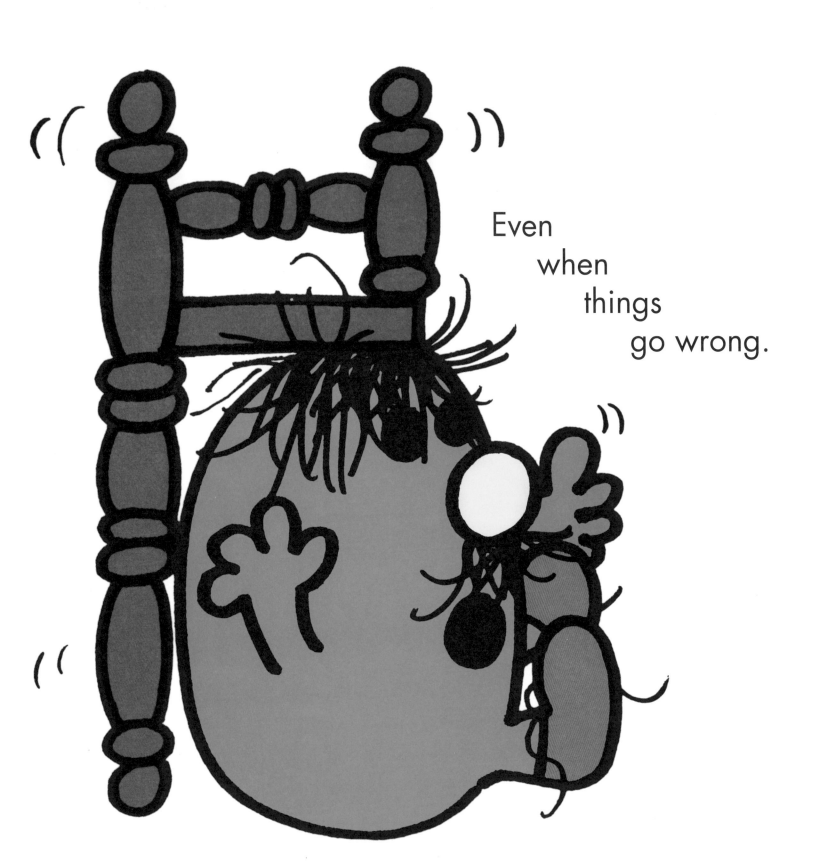

Even
when
things
go wrong.

We often have lots of questions.

But my teacher always has an answer,
no matter how silly the question may be.

My teacher has helped me with my writing.

And given me
a love of books.

Sometimes my teacher likes things to be just so.

But when I'm confused, they know
exactly the right way to help.

My teacher is always there to look after us.

They have nurtured me and helped me to grow.

I know how proud and happy
my teacher is when I try my best.

They are head and shoulders above the rest.

Now the time has come for my teacher to take a break.

You're the best teacher ever and you deserve it— we're your biggest fans!

MY TEACHER

My teacher is most like ....

My favorite book this year was ....

....

I enjoyed learning about ....

I have gotten better at ....

....

My teacher is very kind because ....

....

They will remember when I ....

....

My teacher enjoys ....

I want to say thank you for ....

....

This is a picture
of my teacher and me:

by ....

age ....